Federico AND the Wolf

Rebecca J. Gomez

Illustrated by Elisa Chavarri

Clarion Books | Houghton Mifflin Harcourt | Boston New York

CLARION BOOKS
3 Park Avenue, New York, New York 10016

Clarion Books is an imprint of Houghton Mifflin Harcourt Publishing Company.

hmhbooks.com

The illustrations in this book were done in Photoshop.
The text was set in Chaparral Pro.
Book design by Sharismar Rodriguez

Library of Congress Cataloging-in-Publication Data
Names: Gomez, Rebecca J., author | Chavarri, Elisa, illustrator.
Title: Federico and the wolf / Rebecca J. Gomez ; illustrated by Elisa Chavarri.
Description: Boston ; New York : Clarion Books, Houghton Mifflin Harcourt, [2020]
Summary: A modern retelling of Little Red Riding Hood in which Federico rides
his bicycle to the market for Abuelo's groceries, then stands up to a hungry wolf.
Includes a recipe for pico de gallo and glossary of Spanish terms.
Identifiers: LCCN 2019007314 | ISBN 9781328567789 (hardcover picture book)
Subjects: | CYAC: Stories in rhyme. | Wolves—Fiction. | Grandfathers—Fiction.
Classification: LCC PZ8.3.G585613 Fed 2020 | DDC [E]—dc23
LC record available at https://lccn.loc.gov/2019007314

Manufactured in China
SCP 10 9 8 7 6 5 4 3 2
4500818073

To Jake
—R.J.G

Para Marcel, mi Papucho
—E.C.

Once upon a modern time
a boy named Federico
left to buy ingredients
to make the perfect pico.

"¡Cuidado!" called his mama
as he pedaled toward the shops.
"Mind Abuelo's grocery list,
and don't make other stops!"

Past the buildings, cars, and cabs
young Federico scurried,
until he reached the marketplace
where people browsed, unhurried.

He filled the basket on his bike
with romas, herbs, and limes,
jalepeños, onions,
and a peck of Anaheims.

He added garlic, pickles, bread,
and other market goods,
then pedaled through the city park
and deep into the woods.

FLORES
2 Por 1

A fallen branch had blocked the path,
so Rico stopped his ride.
With steady force he pushed and budged
the barrier aside.

"¡Hola!" called un lobo,
catching Rico unaware.
"I see you've packed a hefty lunch.
Ya got some grub to spare?"

"Sorry, lobo," Rico said.
"I must be on my way.
I have to be at Grandpa's shop
by twelve o'clock today."

Federico grabbed his bike
and left the wolf behind.
(Little did he know the wolf
had other plans in mind.)

La tienda was deserted.
Rico listened . . . not a sound.
The sign said CLOSED. And what were those?
Some paw prints on the ground?

Federico peeked inside,
alarmed by what he saw.
A figure waved him over
with a large and furry paw.

De

"¿Abuelo?" whispered Federico,
pulling off his hood.

"Yes, it's me, but I can't see.
Come closer, if you would."

"¡Ay! I think you need a shave.
Your beard has grown so thick!"

"You think so?" said el lobo.
"Steady grooming does the trick."

"Your arms have gotten grande!"

"My new workout's made me strong."

"New dentures, too?"

"They help me chew
because they're sharp . . .
and long!"

By now the wolf was drooling.
"All this chatter's getting old.
I'm hungry, bub. I need some grub
before I pass out cold."

"Okay," said Rico. "Let me see.
I've brought your favorite treats.
Whole grain bread, a cabbage head,
a jar of pickled beets."

El lobo's nose began to twitch.
"Mi niño, here's the deal.
Set those yucky things aside,
and I'll make you my meal!"

He bounded from la silla
with a grunting, growling shout,
but Rico tossed some chili powder
straight into his snout.

The wolf inhaled. He sniffed. He snuffed.
He itched and twitched and wheezed.
He tried to wipe his drippy nose,
but *ah-ah-ah-ah* sneezed!

Federico ducked and dashed,
then rummaged through his sack.

"Not so fast, you tasty tyke.
I haven't had my snack!"

But Rico quickly plotted.
When the wolf's mouth opened wide,
he grabbed un habanero,
and he jammed it deep inside!

El lobo gulped. He gagged and coughed.
His ojos blazed bright red.
Steam was puffing out his ears.
"I need to dunk my head!"

He hurtled through la puerta
with a shrieking, gasping scream
and dashed as fast as he could go
toward the distant stream.

"¡Ayuda!" cried Abuelo
from inside a bolted box.
Rico found him safe and snug
in just his shorts and socks.

"¡Gracias!" He scrambled out
with shouts of pride and joy.
"I thought that wolf would do us in,
but you prevailed, my boy!"

They cleaned the mess (and Gramps got dressed),
then shared a bit of lunch.

"How about we make a sauce
that packs a special punch?"

They chopped and diced, used lots of spice,
and simmered sauce all night,
then bottled their concoction:
Wolf's Bane Salsa—extra bite!

THE PERFECT PICO

Pico is short for "pico de gallo" (PEE-ko deh GUY-oh), which literally means "rooster's beak." It is a type of fresh salsa made with roma tomatoes, onions, and jalapeños. Some people prefer to use Anaheim peppers in place of jalapeños for a milder flavor. But either way you make it, this pico is perfecto!

½ small onion, chopped

1 small jalapeño, seeded and finely chopped

4 roma tomatoes, diced

1 garlic clove, minced

Pinch of salt

1 teaspoon lime or lemon juice

2 tablespoons chopped fresh cilantro

Mix all ingredients in a medium-size bowl. Chill for 15 to 30 minutes before serving. Enjoy as a taco topping or with your favorite tortilla chips.

Can you find these Spanish words and phrases in the story?

CUIDADO (kwee-DAH-doh): Care or caution
When Federico's mama says, "¡Cuidado!" she is
telling him to be careful.

ABUELO (ah-BWEH-lo): Grandfather or Grandpa

CHURROS (CHOO-rohs): A stick-shaped pastry that is fried
and coated in cinnamon sugar ¡Delicioso!

FLORES (FLOR-ehs): Flowers

HOLA (OH-la): Hello

UN LOBO (oon LO-bo): A wolf

LA TIENDA (la tee-EN-da): The shop, or the store
La tienda is where Abuelo sells his salsas.

DE TODO UN POCO (deh TOH-doh oon PO-co): The sign above
Abuelo's shop means "a bit of everything."

¡AY! (EYE): An expression of surprise, similar to "whoa!"

GRANDE (GRAN-deh): Big

MI NIÑO (me NEEN-yo): My boy

LA SILLA (la SEE-ya): The chair

UN HABANERO (oon ah-bah-NER-oh): A small,
very spicy hot pepper

OJOS (OH-hohs): Eyes

LA PUERTA (la PWER-ta): The door

¡AYUDA! (ah-YOU-da): Help!

GRACIAS (GRA-see-ahs): Thank you

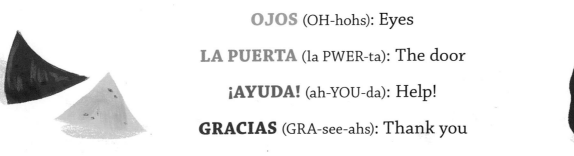